Paul and Sebastian

A Story by René Escudié
Illustrated by Ulises Wensell

Translated by Roderick Townley

A C R A N K Y N E L L B O O K

KM Kane/Miller Book Publishers

Brooklyn, New York & La Jolla, California

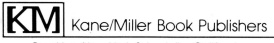

Paul's mother lived in a green trailer with blue curtains.

Sebastian's mother lived in a blue apartment with green curtains.

  Sebastian's mother would look out the apartment window and say:
  "How can anyone live in a trailer? It's so small, and cold, and dark. It smells of earth and dog hairs. It smells awful!"

Paul's mother would look out the window of the trailer and say:

"How can anybody live in an apartment? It doesn't move, it just sits there. It's too hot, and it smells of cleaning fluid and bleach. It smells awful!"

Paul went looking for Sebastian.

Sebastian's mother opened the door of the blue apartment and asked him:

"Who are you? Where do you live?"

Paul replied:

"My name is Paul. I live in the green trailer with the blue curtains."

Sebastian's mother said:

"Go away! You don't live in an apartment like us. You don't smell of cleaning fluid or heating oil, or steak, or noodles. You smell bad."

Sebastian went looking for Paul.

Paul's mother opened the door of the green trailer and asked him:

"Who are you? Where do you live?"

Sebastian answered:

"My name is Sebastian. I live in the blue apartment with the green curtains."

Paul's mother said:

"Go away! You don't live in a trailer like us. You don't smell of earth and dog hairs. You don't smell of stew or apples. You smell bad."

Sebastian's mother told Sebastian:
"I don't want you playing with that boy from the trailer anymore."

Paul's mother said to Paul:
"I don't want you playing with that boy from the apartment anymore."

So when Paul and Sebastian went to school, they didn't walk on the same side of the street. In the playground, they didn't play together. They were very obedient.

At night, Sebastian would tell his mother:
"I didn't play with Paul today."
And Paul would say to his mother:
"I didn't play with Sebastian today."

And both mothers said:
"That's good. They are not our kind of people."

One day, the whole school went on an outing in the country. The children picked flowers in a field beside a little stream.

In the middle of the field there was a little cabin with a red roof and red walls, red shutters and a red door.

All at once it started to rain. Plop! plip! plop! It rained harder and harder and kept it up a long long time.

All the school children ran for shelter under the trees.

15

All except Sebastian and Paul who took refuge under the eaves of the red cabin, where the rain kept falling on them anyway.

They huddled against the door. Suddenly it opened, and they fell inside the red cabin, onto the red floor.

The walls were red, the chairs were red, the bed was red,

and the table was yellow with a bouquet of flowers right in the middle.

Paul and Sebastian both went to sit down in a corner—of course, not the same corner.

They looked at each other but they didn't say anything, they didn't play anything, they didn't do anything.

They didn't even hear the rain stop or the other children leave. They didn't notice the night coming on, or the moon rising in the sky.

Suddenly, at the same moment, they both cried out: "We're lost!"

Then they laughed, because they'd spoken at the same time.

Paul said: "It's all right, it's like being in a trailer. Don't be scared."

Sebastian answered: "It's all right, it's like being in an apartment. Don't be scared."

"Do you know the way back?" asked Paul.
"No," said Sebastian, "it's too dark out. We'll have to wait until morning."

Paul had a piece of salami in his pocket, and he shared it with Sebastian.
Sebastian had a chunk of chocolate, and he shared it with Paul.

In a drawer, they found part of a candle and a box of matches. They lit the candle and ate the chocolate and the salami.

Then the candle went out.

Paul said: "Aren't you cold? Here, take my sweater."

Sebastian said: "Aren't you cold? Here, take my jacket."

So Paul put on Sebastian's jacket, and Sebastian put on Paul's sweater.

Then they climbed into the red bed together and fell asleep.

Much, much later, in the middle of the night, there were noises outside. But the boys heard nothing. They were fast asleep.

There were people, lots of people, searching in the field, searching by the stream, searching under the trees.

Sebastian's mother was there, calling out: "Sebastian! Sebastian!"

Paul's mother was there, too, and she shouted: "Paul! Paul!"

Paul's mother and Sebastian's mother went into the little house. Inside it was pitch black. They felt their way around till they came to the bed, and there they could feel the two little boys.

Sebastian's mother exclaimed: "That's Sebastian's jacket! That's my Sebastian!"

Paul's mother cried out: "That's Paul's sweater! That's my little Paul!"

Sebastian's mother returned to the apartment with the boy in her arms. Because of the storm, there had been a power failure, so she couldn't see anything inside.

Sebastian's mother undressed the little boy, rocked him in her arms, laid him down, and kissed him.

All the while he remained asleep.

Paul's mother arrived at the trailer with the
boy in her arms. There was no more oil for the
lamp, so she couldn't see anything inside.

Paul's mother undressed the little boy, rocked
him in her arms, laid him down, and kissed him.

All the while he remained asleep.

The next morning, Paul's mother and Sebastian's mother went to wake up their children.

But in Paul's little bed there was Sebastian fast asleep!

And in Sebastian's bed, there was Paul, dreaming away!

Paul's mother raced to the window of the trailer. And Sebastian's mother ran to the window of the apartment.

They looked at each other, and then, at the same time, they smiled.

Now, Sebastian and Paul play together, laugh together, dream together
in the green trailer with the blue curtains,
and in the blue apartment with the green curtains.